PETER PAN

RETOLD BY CAROL OTTOLENGHI
ILLUSTRATED BY SHELLEY BRANT

Made in the USA.   ISBN 978-1-4838-4105-2
01-234177784

KU-246-391

Long ago, the Darling family lived in London. Every night, Mrs. Darling told her three children, Wendy, John, and Michael, exciting stories about an island with pirates and Indians. Sometimes, she felt as if someone else was listening to her stories. One night, she saw him!

Mrs. Darling laid a trap to catch the sneaky listener. She did not catch him, but she did catch his shadow! She showed it to her husband, Mr. Darling.

"Very good, my dear," he said. "It must have been a burglar. Well, he won't be back. You scared him off."

Two nights later, Mr. and Mrs. Darling went to a party.

"Oh, Mother!" said Wendy. "You look beautiful. When may I wear a dress like that?"

"You may wear one when you are all grown up," said Mrs. Darling. "Just don't grow up too fast." Then, she and Mr. Darling kissed their children and left.

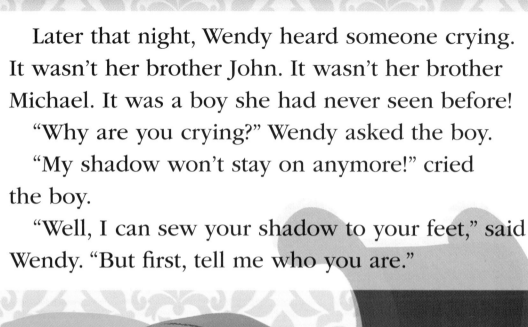

Later that night, Wendy heard someone crying. It wasn't her brother John. It wasn't her brother Michael. It was a boy she had never seen before!

"Why are you crying?" Wendy asked the boy.

"My shadow won't stay on anymore!" cried the boy.

"Well, I can sew your shadow to your feet," said Wendy. "But first, tell me who you are."

"I am Peter Pan!" said the boy.

Wendy finished sewing on the shadow, and Peter Pan leapt to his feet. "Thank you!" he said. "I flew here. As a reward for helping me, you and your brothers can fly with me to Neverland."

He sprinkled Wendy, John, and Michael with fairy dust from his friend Tinker Bell. And what do you know? They could fly!

As they flew high above the other houses, Wendy asked, "Why were you at our house, Peter?"

"I like to hear your mother's stories," said Peter. "Do you know any stories?"

"Of course," said Wendy.

"Then, you can be Mother to the Lost Boys and tell us stories. Look," Peter pointed, "Neverland!"

Tinker Bell felt jealous. "Peter is my friend," she said to herself. "Not Wendy's."

Tinker Bell told the Lost Boys that Wendy was a giant bird. "Peter wants you to shoot it down with arrows," she said. So, the Lost Boys knocked Wendy out of the sky.

Peter was furious! "This girl was going to be our mother and tell us stories," he told them. The Lost Boys felt bad. They built Wendy a house to stay in.

When Wendy was feeling better, they all set off to rescue Tiger Lily, the Indian princess, who had been captured by pirates.

The captain of the pirates was Captain Hook. He hated the Lost Boys, Peter Pan, and crocodiles. Long ago, he had been holding a clock when a crocodile jumped out of the water and bit off his hand. Now, Captain Hook had a hook for a hand, and the crocodile sounded like *tick-tock, tick-tock*!

While Peter and Hook fought, Wendy and the Lost Boys rescued Tiger Lily. Captain Hook slashed Peter with his hook before Peter could get away.

Life at Neverland was exciting, but John and Michael were homesick. "We miss Mother and Father," they told Wendy.

"We are going home, and the Lost Boys are coming with us," Wendy told Peter. "You may come, too."

"No!" Peter yelled. "I would have to grow up!"
Wendy gave Peter some medicine. "This will make your cut better. Make sure you take it."

Wendy and the boys left, but they did not get far! The pirates captured them one by one as they climbed out of the tree house.

"Take them to the ship!" Captain Hook told the other pirates.

Then, Captain Hook snuck into the tree house and poured poison into Peter's medicine!

"This will be wonderful," Captain Hook told Wendy. "The boys shall be pirates, and you shall be our mother."

"Never!" Wendy yelled. "Peter Pan will rescue us."

"No, he won't," said Captain Hook. "I poisoned his medicine. Very soon, Peter Pan will be dead!"

Tinker Bell heard this. "I must warn Peter!" she said to herself.

Tinker Bell sped to the tree house. She broke the medicine bottle and told Peter what was happening. "We must rescue them!" Peter cried.

But Captain Hook was very angry at Wendy and the boys. "If you will not be our mother and tell us stories, then the boys must walk the plank!" he said.

Suddenly, there was a loud *tick-tock, tick-tock*.

"No!" cried Captain Hook. "It is the crocodile. It has come back to eat the rest of me."

"I hope the crocodile is hungry!" cried Peter Pan, as he jumped onto the deck.

Tinker Bell sprinkled the other pirates with fairy dust. They floated into the air and could not help their captain.

Peter Pan and Captain Hook wrestled back and forth. Finally, Peter gave a huge push…and pushed Hook overboard!

Peter and Tinker Bell took Wendy, John, Michael, and all of the Lost Boys to the Darlings' home.

"We are glad you came back," cried Mrs. Darling. "We missed you so much."

"May the Lost Boys stay with us?" Wendy asked.

"Of course," said Mr. Darling.

Peter never came to stay with them. But sometimes he would visit…

...when Mrs. Darling was telling stories.

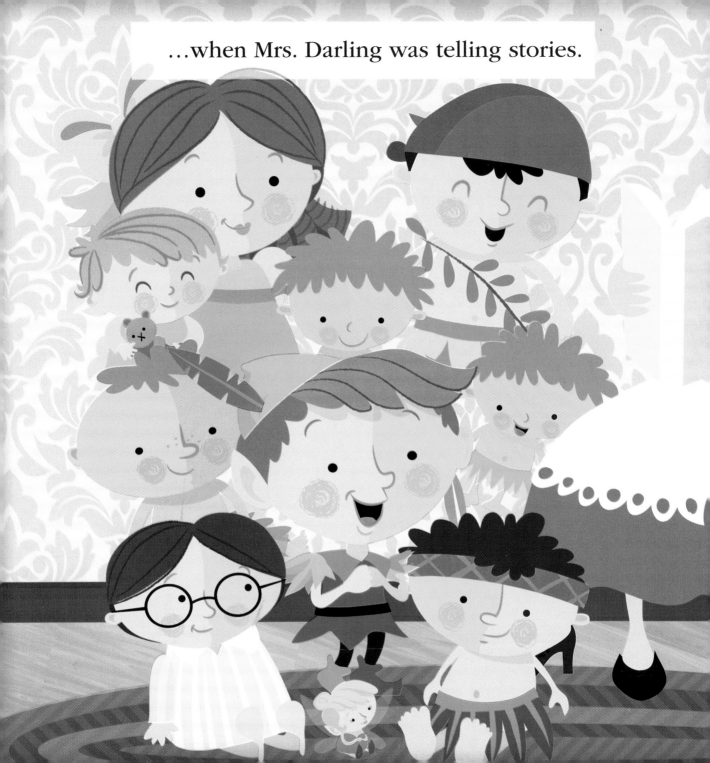